PAPA
PENGUIN

Lindsay Camp

Momoko Abe

ANDERSEN PRESS

At bedtime, Sam feels a bit sad.
His dad isn't home yet, so he won't
be able to tell Sam a story.

Sam's dad is brilliant at telling stories.
He makes them up himself. Sam's favourites
are about dinosaurs with superpowers.

But tonight, Sam's dad is late. So no made-up story for Sam.

Just as he climbs into bed, Sam hears something. He hears the front door opening, and big, heavy feet pounding up the stairs, two at a time.

"Phew!" says Sam's dad, bursting
into the room. "Just made it in time."

"Mm," says Sam, quietly.

"What's up?" asks his dad, sitting down on the bed. "Are you OK?"

"Yes," says Sam.

"Then why the long face?"

"I thought you weren't going to be home in time to tell me a story."

"But I am," says Sam's dad.

"So there's no need to look sad.

"No," says Sam. But he still sounds a bit sad.

"I know what will cheer you up," says his dad. "A story about Captain Triceratops!"

"No," says Sam. "Not today. I want a different story."

Sam's dad looks surprised.

"OK. What about?"

"You decide," says Sam.

His dad thinks for a moment, rubbing his chin. "All right," he says, "I'm going to tell you a story about... a penguin."

"Did the penguin have
any superpowers?" asks Sam.
"No," says his dad.
"Or was he a world champion at anything?"

"No, he was just an ordinary penguin. An ordinary daddy penguin — Papa Penguin."

"Well, what did he do?" asks Sam. "He must have done something, or there wouldn't be a proper story."

"Yes," says Sam's dad. "He did do something. Something amazing. Shall I tell you what it was?"

"OK," says Sam, snuggling down and closing his eyes.

"Well, this Papa Penguin had an egg."

"Did he lay the egg?" asks Sam, opening his eyes again.

Sam's dad laughs. "That *would* be amazing.

No, it was the mummy penguin
who did that. But as soon as she'd
laid the egg, she went off to sea,
to find some fish to eat."

"So she left the egg with the daddy penguin, to look after?"
"That's right," says Sam's dad. "And do you know what he did with it?"
"No. What?"

"He balanced it on top of his feet, so that it wouldn't get too cold on the ice." Now Sam laughs. "But how could Papa Penguin walk, if he had an egg balanced on his feet?"

"He couldn't. He could hardly move at all. All he could do was stand there, and try his best to keep the egg warm, so that the penguin chick inside would hatch out safely."

"But what did he have to eat?" says Sam. "Did the mummy penguin come back with some fish?"

"No," says Sam's dad. "She was away at sea, for weeks and weeks. So the daddy penguin got very hungry. Very, very hungry indeed. And very, very cold, too. Poor Papa Penguin!"

"Did anyone help him look after the egg?" says Sam.
"No," says his dad. "He didn't need any help. It was his egg, so it was his job to look after it."

"So what happened then?" says Sam.
"Nothing," says his dad.
"Nothing?" says Sam.
"Something must have happened. Did aliens land on the ice?"

"No," says his dad. "No aliens. Papa Penguin just stood there, with the egg balanced on his feet, trying his best to keep the chick inside warm and safe, while the icy blizzards blew and blew, harder and harder, colder and colder."

"And then what happened?" says Sam, yawning sleepily.

"Still nothing. Papa Penguin just went on standing there in the freezing winds,

day after day,
night after night,

Z
Z
Z

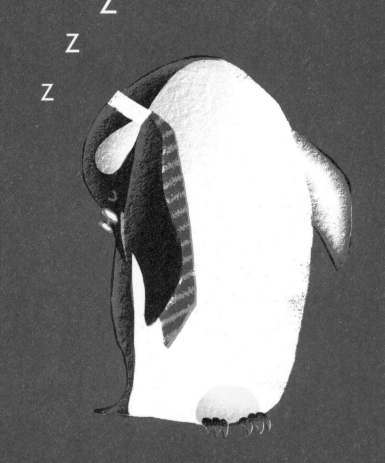

for weeks and weeks,
hardly moving at all,

and getting hungrier
and hungrier. Until...

at last, the egg hatched,
and he saw his chick."

Sam can hardly keep his eyes open.
"Was the chick magical?
Could it fly faster than
a supersonic jet?"
"No, penguins can't fly!
It was just an ordinary
penguin chick, all
covered in fluff."
"Was it a boy or
a girl?" asks Sam.
"It was a boy. A
beautiful baby
boy-chick."

"And then what happened?"
says Sam. But his voice sounds
muffled and far away.
"And then the mummy penguin
came back," says Sam's dad,

"and it was the hungry daddy penguin's turn to swim out to sea and catch some fish.

But of course, he came back as soon
as he could. Because Papa Penguin
loved his beautiful boy-chick."
Sam doesn't say anything at all.

"Night night," whispers his dad, pulling up Sam's quilt to keep him warm. But Sam isn't quite asleep yet.

"Dad," he murmurs into his pillow, "will you tell me about
Papa Penguin and his boy-chick again tomorrow?"
"Of course I will," says his dad. "I promise."

Did you know that in this story, Papa Penguin behaves just like emperor penguins in the real world?

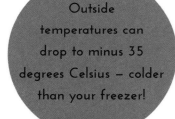

2 Afterwards she travels back to the ocean to find food, leaving the papa penguin to look after the egg.

Outside temperatures can drop to minus 35 degrees Celsius — colder than your freezer!

1 **Emperor penguins** live in Antarctica in the southern hemisphere. At the start of their autumn, once they've reached their breeding grounds, each female penguin lays one egg before carefully transferring it to her mate by rolling it with their feet and beaks.

The eggs are pear-shaped, pale greenish-white, and about the size of a mango.

3 Papa penguins have to be extra vigilant, because an egg can only withstand the freezing temperatures on the ice for 1-2 minutes. They have no food during this time so the papa penguins may lose almost half of their body weight.

4 For around nine long, wintry weeks, the papa emperor penguins huddle together to keep their eggs safe and warm on their feet, covered only by a fold of skin — never letting the egg touch the ice — while they wait for them to hatch.

Penguin parents feed their chicks with regurgitated fish, squid and crustaceans.

6 When the mother comes home, the male is ravenously hungry, and leaves for the ocean to find food for himself and their chick.

Penguins can recognise their own chick by the sound of its call.

5 The eggs begin to hatch after a couple of months, but the female penguins won't return for about three months. The male penguins endure such intense cold and hardship, and sometimes danger with predators close by, it is a true testament to the bond between the fathers and their chicks.

7 For the next three months, the male and female penguins take it in turn to stay and look after their baby chick and go to the ocean to feed, until the chicks are old enough to be left on their own. Soon the chicks grow waterproof feathers and can forage for themselves at sea, but they never forget the special bond they have with their papas.

For Finley and Marlowe, our beautiful boy-chicks – L.C.

For my father – M.A.

First published in Great Britain in 2021 by Andersen Press Ltd.,

20 Vauxhall Bridge Road, London SW1V 2SA.

Text copyright © Lindsay Camp, 2021. Illustrations copyright © Momoko Abe, 2021.

The rights of Lindsay Camp and Momoko Abe to be identified as the author

and illustrator of this work have been asserted by them in

accordance with the Copyright, Designs and Patents Act, 1988.

All rights reserved.

Printed and bound in China.

1 3 5 7 9 10 8 6 4 2

British Library Cataloguing in Publication Data available.

ISBN 978 1 78344 976 7